WHAT IS TO COME

STEPHEN JENSEN

ISBN 978-1-0980-9708-0 (paperback)
ISBN 978-1-0980-9709-7 (digital)

Christian Faith Publishing, Inc.
832 Park Avenue
Meadville, PA 16335
www.christianfaithpublishing.com

Printed in the United States of America

Preface

If it was not for God, the Holy Spirit, my Father, family, and my brothers and sisters in Christ, this book would have never happened. I hope that you enjoy engaging the ideas within this small book as much as I enjoyed writing them.

What Is To Come

Greg walked down the eroded avenue. It paralleled the great grassy woodland, which was broken only by the occasional tumbled statuary. How he got here was no longer important. He had lost everything so he could be here. Why dwell on the journey? He had his purpose, and now he could fulfill it. The cost had been great. He ambled down the road if it could even be called that anymore, looking for the temple.

Years ago, he had been an officer in an army. He had been a full-throated patriot, family man, and a Christian. Now he was simply a Christian. The Nation had collapsed in a gout of flame and smoke as it had arisen. His family had died in the final invasion when every citizen became a soldier. But even so, this simply made subjugation unpalatable. The invasion still unwound the fabric of the people of Greg's land. It would never be woven back together. The warp and woof that had made the original garment of people, law and ideal possible had long been lost in sexual appetite, avarice, and apathy.

There had still been noblemen and noblewomen who were able to scrape together pockets of order, but the enemy knew that this great power would not rise again. At least, this is why Greg figured they did not attack anymore. They could make deals for resources with the pockets easier than they could force the pockets to do their bidding. Besides, if the enemy really did try and subject the remnants, could that not provide the very force necessary to reanimate the dead Nation?

Greg did not ponder these things for long. The thoughts always caused his blood to boil. He had been willing to give his life for his people and their ideals. In the end, the Nation destroyed itself and all he loved with it. But he had survived.

His company of infantry had been at the front, had been part of the initial battles where the enemy was struck hard and recoiled. Those had been bloody, horrible actions. Iron and flesh make for a dark poetry that only enraptures the insane and Satan. His company was pulled back for rest and to allow other soldiers to win their glory by flame and blood. The enemy recovered quickly during this rotation and caught Greg's fellow units off guard. The line collapsed, and though reformed, would never push forward again. Instead, the higher-ups conducted a series of *tactical withdrawals*.

Greg's people never lost, at least not like this. The pressure back at home mounted on the Capitol. The puppeteers, who had no more strings to pull, ordered their forces home, prepared for invasion, and disappeared into bunkers. Those who they ruled over were left to hope the enemy would deal with them kindly.

Greg was sent to the place he had been born. The big wigs assumed soldiers would better defend their places of first breath. As in many things, the big wigs did this without giving thought to the most important thing to a soldier—his family. The soldiers were promised their families would be safe; they were on installations designed to fend off attacks.

Two problems arose in Greg's mind when he had read this in the letter his commander sent to reassure a battered force. One, this Nation had not been invaded for centuries. Military bases were not designed to resist much more than lone wolf attacks and small civil demonstrations. Second, the very fact they were military installations made them the likeliest targets to be hit first and to be hit without mercy.

And so it happened, that the post Greg had served was totally demolished, nothing within its boundaries neither beast or human was left alive. No survivors meant Greg would mercifully never learn the horrors those he loved endured before death. Other than that, he was devastated. When the enemy reached his town, he and his men defended with such ferocity that the foe was turned away, never to return. Greg's place of birth was not worth great loss.

In the grand scheme of things, its existence affected nothing of the enemy's plans. The bigger cities did not fare so well. The men who defended the urban centers had long ago lost their fervor for God and country, amongst the debauchery of their places of birth. They quickly retreated and melted into the countryside, leaving the once gleaming metropolises to be burned to the ground.

It took about three months for most of the great cities to fall. The Capitol lasted a year. Then the politicians and powerful were paraded, hung, and buried. When the news reached Greg, he was numb from everything. For some reason, this final event brought a burning desire to truly understand how this happened. Not just the rumors and official reports, he would go to the source of the Nation's power and get the truth from documents among the ruins.

His journey across the Nation would have broken most men in their right mind and turned them from their way. Lucky for Greg, he had not been in his right mind since he received the report of the raising of his garrison and the certain death of all that he had loved.

Men and women wandered aimlessly in towns without real purpose. Many of these places had come into existence to house the families of men and women who had worked in the cities. Without the cities, these people had no purpose, no way of surviving. There was a great amount of pilfering, and those who had jarred goods or preserved foods were kings. At one point, Greg witnessed a grown man chasing down and beating a boy who had tried to make off with a bag of oats.

Greg had beat the man, and as he turned to offer the boy protection, he watched the boy run away with the oats. In this time, goodness seemed impossible. Greg loved the Lord, but his faith had faded. He had no Bible and no fellowship. Scripture had been outlawed for a while before the war. People of the faith could not gather publicly. Horrible displays were made of those caught practicing the faith. But the faith had grown in these troubled times. It seemed the harder the Capitol tried to suppress Christ; the more people flocked to Him.

Greg stumbled over a paving stone. He looked around at the desolate city, broken statues, and colonnades. A great people's splendor spent. He saw among the ruins an old lady. She sat at the foot of the statue of a headless soldier riding on his noble steed. She seemed to be slumped over in slumber.

It was a warm day, not hot, with a pleasant breeze. It was a day that reminds one that life goes on no matter the horrors that humanity wrought upon itself. Greg decided to speak with the old woman; perhaps she would know how to find what he sought. Besides, this ruinous place was perfectly lonesome, and he wanted to talk to anybody at this point. It had been months since he had any form of interaction with another person.

As he drew closer to the headless cavalryman, the lady stirred at his footfalls. As she raised her wizened head, she flashed her visitor a toothless smile.

"What business have you with me, young man? Surely, you do not find yourself affected by my charms!" She cackled, obviously wandering down paths of madness.

Greg was having second thoughts about his decision. "Nope, but I was hoping you could help me find my way."

"I am lost myself, young man. The difference is I cannot change my way any longer, my finish line is set, and I will be quickly reaching my final destination." Another toothless smile. But she spoke with some intelligence, much more than he would expect from an old woman with no teeth.

"The directions I need have very little to do with where I am going when I die. I am simply looking for the official archives." At this point, he had reached the base of the statue with no head, before the seated woman. He felt he should sit, that standing would be rude. At the same time, he was afraid if he did sit down, he may never get up again. He suddenly felt the overwhelming weariness of his long wandering, both physically and in his spirit.

"Whether it be an earthly destination or a spiritual one, it still affects your final destination. But I do not mean to wax esoteric with a stranger. My name is Prisce. And as you can imagine, a time like this one would drive most to madness, I simply went one step further, into philosophy," another cackle.

"What is your name, young man?" Greg rolled his eyes; his limbs were growing heavier by the moment. Was this Prisce trying to draw him from his goal? Was he willing to leave her and continue to wander the immensity of the Capitol without direction? He saw greater hope, even if greater risk in guidance from this strange creature.

"My name is Greg. Now, can you point me on my way, Prisce, or should I be going?"

"I know the way, Greg. But we are far from it. Besides, despite the abandoned quality of these ruins, they are filled with men and women turned to wickedness through desperation. It is not safe to move about at night, and evening is upon us. Come with me and have shelter, rest this night, eat a decent meal, and we will find these archives you seek first thing in the morning." She spoke with knowledge, honesty, and kindness. Greg had already given in to her, and whether there were people in the ruins, his sudden exhaustion made it folly to test the validity of Prisce's statements.

Greg said, "All right, but know that I served our Nation as a soldier, an officer, and will not be easy to subdue if this be a trap."

Prisce replied, "Foolish Greg, you come to me, and the fire long left this old shell, and you certainly have little meat on your bones. I have no reason to betray you. But all the same, there are ways that you would have no power to resist, even though you were a soldier, for me to trap you. Now, follow me, and we will be safe before the sun sets and full before the moon rises."

They wandered, seeming almost to meander, first past colonnades of marble, then those of clay, and finally, buildings with awnings held up by simple wood posts. The buildings reflected the cheapening quality of their entrance ways. Weeds and vines grew in obvious disregard of the city around them.

They reached a large four-story building, with designs pressed in its facing to give its drab brown nature some cheer. Built up against it was a small shed, clay tiles of deep red upon its roof. A small fountain bubbled in the courtyard, which the shed thrust itself into, not knowing it no longer had a purpose.

"To the shed, young man. It is small but unsuspecting and one of the only places left near running water." No cackle followed, just a serious face at the mournful chuckling of life-giving water. Prisce swiftly opened the door to the shed, ushering Greg through, and then following him in, closed and bolted it. The final rays of sunshine passed through a slit of what had once been a window looking out on the courtyard. Someone had bricked it up against urban bandits, Greg assumed.

It was a single room, with a hard-packed dirt floor, a humble hearth, and some bedding near the hearth. The hearth was cold but clean, no ash left from the merry fires that typically inhabited it. A pile of wood items, from building beams to small tiles, sat nearer the door. Other than that, the shed was bare. But it was still better than many of the hovels and abandoned places in which Greg had stayed.

"Sit and make yourself at home. You can use some of the bedding to cushion your rear. I will start the fire and get supper in the pot."

Greg obeyed, pulling a wool blanket and folding it in half and then in half again, to serve as an expedient cushion.

Prisce pried up a previously innocuous tile, revealing storage space underneath. She looked up at Greg with a smile.

"Our little secret." Then she quietly chuckled at herself as she pulled up a pot, knife, flint, dried weeds, and a package that, by the grease stains, seemed to contain a piece of meat. She unwrapped the meat. It was encrusted with pepper and salt and proceeded to cut a quarter. She tossed it in the pot, pulled a vase of water from another hiding place, and filled the pot with water. Then she placed the pot on the fire and slowly stirred.

"How long have you wandered? And for what do you seek?" she asked.

As the room grew darker, the small fire became the sole provider of light. It cast the old woman in relief, making her wrinkles and creases look much deeper than they were.

"I don't know how long I have wandered. I seek to truly know how our great people could have been so terribly defeated."

"Have you no one to love and care for?"

"No, the war took them like everything else." He said this flatly, resisting the screaming darkness that burbled at his declaration.

"Then you and I share a pain. I once had children and grandchildren. We were an old and influential family. So naturally, the enemy murdered them all." She choked, a tear bumping its way from eye to chin across valleys of bereavement. She took a deep breath, stirring the pot after the momentary lapse of control.

"But this, too, has passed. Not too long after, I found this shed. Another had prepared it before the troubles, sensing the coming doom, I guess. It would seem the preparer was swept away by the doom he had planned for. Oh well, his loss was my gain! He, he, he." The water was starting to boil.

She continued, "I flitted about, collecting what scraps of wood and food I could find. Part of me simply wished to give it all up, to die, and face the dark ignorance of death I thought awaited us all. Then I found amongst the scraps a series of pages, writings from those trouble-making followers of Christ. I had nothing but time and loneliness, so I started to read. It was unlike anything I had ever known. My whole life had been about me. Even my religion was in the end about how I had to be a good girl.

"But in these pages, I learned of man's true condition, broken pots that, like any pot, could not remake themselves. Only their potter could do that. I learned this is exactly what the potter wanted to do. But to heal his creation. He had to become his creation, he had to be a pot unbroken so he could be broken in place of his pottery and thereby mend them. His name was Jesus, do you know of him? Besides the lies told by the authorities and wealthy fools now swept away as so many sparks from a forge?"

Greg looked up, having been staring between his knees at the ground, totally exhausted. The old woman stared at him with intensity that made conviction swell in his heart. He did know Jesus, had lived for him and then turned from him when he should have been most heavily leaning into him.

"I know him, but I have wandered away from him since I lost my family."

"How interesting. By losing my family, I found Jesus. Losing yours, you left Him." She turned away and stirred more vigorously.

"Is it only meat for the pot?" Greg did not have the power to offer much resistance to the emotional damn ready to burst. Silence followed, with the bubbling stew, the crackle of the fire, and the odd clank of Prisce's stirring breaking it. A smell began to fill the room that was pleasant to Greg's empty stomach. Meat was indeed the rarest of luxuries in a world on fire.

When his eyes opened again, he found the room was now black but for the merry hearth. He could feel the cold seeping through the walls, making the fire all the more cheering. Prisce noticed his waking. She had removed the pot from the flames and had split the meat on two plates, one of which she offered to Greg. "It's not much, but more than most will eat this night."

He took the plate, pulled a knife from his pocket, cutting the meat and shoveling it to his mouth. He ate it quickly, finished, and tilted the plate to drink all the gravy. He sat back and watched the old lady savor every bite. He imagined part of this was a necessity. Owing to her having no teeth and so, only able to eat small bits at a time. As he watched her, he realized that at one time, she must have been a real beauty, but the war had taken even that from her.

When she had about half her meal left, she looked at Greg. "Tell me about those you loved. I know it is painful, but a wound cannot be healed simply by being ignored. It must be dressed and cleaned."

Greg just stared in horror. How could he refuse her? She had fed and sheltered him. This was the least she could ask of him; this was the most she could ask of him.

But her talk of Jesus had cracked the wall he had built around his heart, and water had begun pouring through the widening gap.

"I met Aestas...in wheat fields...outside my home. Border wars...were turning orphans of all good folk. She was dirty, hair full of dust smoke, her face sooty. Her feet were bleeding from crossing miles of open ground. She collapsed in my arms. She stunk, exhausted. So light, I carried her in my arms to my family's house.

"She slept for days. I did not see her again for half a year. I had gone to city for tutelage. I returned... It was fall, the weather had begun to cool. I walked to the front door from the main road. The sun just about to drop, the air crisp, promising a cold night. I saw the house and the most beautiful woman I had ever laid my gaze upon. Her hair long, coppery, flitting in a final evening gasp of chill air. Her eyes flashed green-blue as she turned looking at me, the sun setting them aflame," he paused, relishing the memory of the first sight of his love.

"We had a long courtship. With wars picking up, it was clear I would be a soldier. I spent most of my time gaining the knowledge needed to run the family estate and training for war. As I prepared to move to my first garrison, we married, and in a few years, had two sons and a daughter. My daughter's second birthday came and went while I was deployed for the final battles that would destroy her and all else I loved. She looked so much like Aestas." He sobbed.

"This world is so evil. Nothing is fixed, nothing stays the same. Nothing matters, for in a moment, a single gust blows it away!" raged Greg.

"I must know why our Nation came to ruin, how the Capitol could have been so foolish, to be so strong and then collapse in a seeming fit of stupidity. I am not even sure if what I seek can really be found, but if I don't at least look, I don't think I can finish grieving and find another life to live." He just leaned back and let tears flow. Tears of rage at the Nation he had loved to the point of death. A Nation that, in the end, betrayed him. Tears of sorrow at having lost all he loved, tears of release, as long months of pain were finally acknowledged.

Prisce simply watched. Another tear had fallen from her eye, following a similar path to the previous one. "Oh Greg, all I can say is you speak truly in the absence of God. But since all I loved was taken from me, I have turned to God. He has given me my life back, healed but scarred. I know this is small help now, but remember, in you is the Spirit of God, and now He can begin a new work in you. A work of healing and new life!"

He lifted his head and locked his eyes with hers for a moment in acknowledgment. He could feel a new peace as the day had finished breaking within him. He held back his emotion, his acknowledgment of his pain and tribulation.

"Rest for tonight, Greg. I sleep very little in the shadows of life. I am too close to my eternal rest to care much for earthly slumber. I will take you very early tomorrow to the national archives." Prisce added to the cooking fire, warming the room enough to battle the cool of the night. Greg closed his eyes and fell quickly to deep sleep and dreams of Aestas and their children.

The sun's rays were not even pondering the violation of the Capitol's gloom when Prisce shook Greg from slumber. She had rocked him and then jumped back, knowing a soldier's reflex could prove deadly. Greg rolled onto his feet, grabbing his weapon, and then stood relaxed as he remembered where he was. War changes men—it is like the dog who is constantly beaten, and eventually, he is always tense, seeing only danger in all the things and activities of life. Greg smiled at Prisce.

"Good morning, and I mean it. I have not slept deep enough to dream in a long time. I was afraid of what I would find."

"It would seem you found nothing fearful." Prisce grinned a toothless grin.

"No, I saw what I feared I would, but instead of pain, it brought joy."

"Your family?" Prisce added.

"Yes."

Prisce nodded knowingly.

"I see mine when I sleep now too. But, as I said last night, sleep runs from me as I imagine most young men of weaker constitution than you would." She cackled uproariously. Greg allowed a chuckle. As his eyes swept the shed, he saw another piece of meat on the plate from the evening before.

"We eat then go?"

"Yes, it is not far, and once the sun peeks his head over the building tops, we will be safe enough. You can never be totally safe in the Capitol, but I have a strapping young warrior to protect me!" Greg simply crouched and devoured his meat. Prisce then led him to the fountain so he could wash up, and then they began to walk through the city.

The Capitol was built along a river. Its buildings were many columned, built of marble, and covered with imposing portraits and ancient wisdom. Here and there, a near do-well had painted graffiti curses with explicit scenes between outsized people and simply worked to prove that even the most imposing edifice was but a canvas for the boldly ignorant and bored. It was the greatest city in the Nation. It had been so rich that after multiple sackings, one did not have to search hard for precious metals and bejeweled baubles.

Greg had never been impressed with cities in general, and the Capitol was no exception. It felt heavy, meandering, and meaningless. He loved the country. Wide-open, full of possibility, simply waiting for the human hand to move on it.

The sun began warming the marble quickly, but the air held the previous night's chill. Greg would have preferred to walk in the sun, but Prisce kept them in the shadows, not taking any chances.

Prisce talked, "Day or night, the deeper into the city, the less safe we are. There are great stores left by the Nation that have yet to be eaten. Now that the armies are gone, it is the strongest who gets to eat."

Greg nodded his head; he had seen this reality all along his journey here. Now, he found its greatest expression at the very nexus of it all. Was not the real reason for society to give the weakest the freedom from the tyranny of the strong? But in the last days of the Nation, the powerful cared nothing for liberty or equality, just power.

Prisce stopped before the greatest edifice Greg had ever beheld. Great marble columns, walls, and statues gleaming under a hot sun. The steps leading up were well worn from the many feet that had climbed up to seek, obtain, or beseech power.

"The Senate held court here. A bunch of windbags at the end. Once they were great men, men who built a great Nation." She looked troubled and weary.

"My husband had been a senator. He was corrupt, like the rest. He got the wrong end of a dagger in the end, but he was smart enough to set me up for life. Anyway, there are more answers in there than you could ever ask questions for. I will wait out here. There are no stores here, so no people. The inside of that place is horrible to me."

Prisce sat down in the sun. She looked just as she had the day before when Greg met her; to see such peace in the midst of a fallen people awakened some kind of hope in his heart. It also made him chuckle to see an old, wizened woman sitting against the cool marble of the edifice, as if its only purpose was to give her rest.

Greg continued forward, the hope and humor turning to anticipation and a small part dread. He would soon find his answer or be left to wander the Capitol a haunted and tired soldier. He passed through the columns holding up the great roof. All were carved and ornate, a dead beauty that spoke of the beauty of his people. He continued through the great doorway, the doors long gone. Nearby their charred remains spoke of the chaos when the Capitol had fallen. Rusty brown stains were all that was left of men who had commanded the world's capitols.

There were no bodies, bones, or even shrouds that would hint at clothing. Greg blocked himself from thinking about what had happened to the remains whose blood painted the walls. In a siege, people do horrible things.

As he continued down the corridor, he passed chambers and other corridors branching off the main one—all empty, abandoned, and shadowy. Holes in the ceiling let in golden beams of light that hurt the eyes.

A musty, pleasant, papery smell crossed Greg's nose. He looked down a corridor that seemed to end in total twilight. But the smell told him this was what he was looking for. He walked down the second corridor at a faster clip. It was very dark, damp, and dreary. He did not wish to imagine what might reach out and pull him forever down into the shade of this place. He stopped on the threshold to ensure no one was waiting to catch him unawares. He had moved through the edifice like a cat, but a warrior was always over-cautious.

The room before him was so enormous; he felt dizzy looking at the ceiling. Row upon row of great wood shelves filled with everything ever written in the Nation. The floor was dusty. Here and there, piles of ash indicated spots where desperate men and women had burned who knows what, knowledge simply to keep warm.

Greg did not know where to begin. His entire existence since the Nation's defeat had been reactionary, no real thought or planning had been involved. Now, he was where he had wanted to be, and nothing indicated where he could find "reasons why we lost so horribly, or why we even got into a war in the first place."

As he continued to stare into the dim chamber, he saw a beam of light shining through a hole in what looked to be an impenetrable ceiling. Greg knew better than anyone that human and impenetrable were contradictory terms. Everything man built never amounted to more than children's sandcastles in the surf. Except for man, it is not the sea but his own broken nature that allowed for the destruction of his machinations.

Greg moved quickly, feeling the enormity of the place and feeling suddenly exposed. As he drew closer to the sunlight, it grew to be a great splotch on the ground. Motes of dust and paper fibers glittered in the beam. As Greg reached the spot, he saw a scroll laying unfurled upon a desk, a stylus with dried ink laying at the end of a quickly scrawled statement: "QUID VERUM."

"What is truth?" hollered Greg at the statement. Here, surrounded by all the knowledge Rome could hold under one roof and still, this man had not known truth. Instead, he had ignored it, crushed it, and was destroyed by it. Greg wept.

Reality

The Quant was working overtime. It amazed Jonah how man could always find a way to overwork technology developed to be impossible to overwork. The more space you gave men, the more stuff they made to fill it. It was typically meaningless, useless junk. He put the 3Ds on; he hated the Vert.

Why can't people just be happy with the real world? Suddenly, he was in the midst of a grid pattern. Shapes started to merge the straight lines; light started to flood in from behind him. He seemed to sense a breeze blow; a rustle of leaves flooded his ears. He stood staring into woods, the sun setting on a warm afternoon. He looked up and watched as the first points of light began to fill a darkening sky.

Jonah had to find what was causing the Quant to think so hard. The harder it worked the more power it pulled, the more money the Vert manager was spending. Jonah's job was to calm the storm. He began walking through the woods; the trees were randomly generated to give the feel of uniqueness. When the Verts came online, people figured out the gimmick pretty quick. That was before the Quantum computer. The number of calculations it made was so enormous it had to be measured by milliseconds to get a definable number. It easily deceived those who wandered in its renderings.

But the large number of calculations made it difficult to find errors in the programming. At first, they simply let the errors be. They were so insignificant it did not affect the experience. The errors started piling up. Self-repair programs could not work fast enough. Soon the errors started to manifest as errors in the rendering.

Mountains became black holes; a field of flowers became a battlefield filled with corpses.

Coders were struggling to fix the code. It was so complex that simply finding the group the line of code was in took months. Then someone asked in the umpteenth emergency meeting why the code could not be repaired by manipulating the errors in the Vert.

It was so obvious everyone had looked past it. They designed an AI simulation, but this soon failed, as the corrupted code would begin to cause failure in the AIs. Soon, monstrous apparitions were popping up all over the Vert, causing mayhem and emptying the environment of customers. You can't really enjoy a hike through the mountains when a man covered in blood appears in front of you and pulls a butcher knife.

They started sending in humans. They would go to the last reported sightings, interact with the object or AI in question, and voila, no more error. Typically, the fixer would simply program a solution to the scenario presented. The murderous ghoul was put on trial, the black hole mathematically disproved by a rendering of Einstein and whatever other cleverness could be thought up. It turned out the best fixers were individuals who hated the Vert. Their lack of awe gave them the uncanny ability to grimly shrug off otherwise disturbing scenarios as evidence of the stupidity of the whole system.

This allowed them a level of sarcasm and irony with which they could produce solutions to the conundrums the glitches presented. What was never understood was how resolving a scenario could fix the underlying code. The Vert itself was imbued with AI but extremely simple algorithms. It would not do for the Vert to go and think for itself. The Coders got a taste of what that would be like with the AI repair mess. The consensus was that the underlying program was able to translate situational solutions into code that it then used to repair itself.

The grass was thick and springy. Jonah wasn't wearing his Nostrils, so he was not sure what it smelled like. He imagined it would be very pleasant. As he crossed the eve of the forest, he began to see what the disturbance was. Squirrels hanging from the bows by twine around their necks. A grizzly Christmas decoration they would make. They hung totally limp and were in various stages of decay, some looking as if they would leap back up the bough they hung from, others looking like squirrel balloons filled with rotten gasses.

The most disturbing were the ones that appeared to dance as they were presumably being consumed by maggots. Jonah was now quite glad for his no-Nostril policy. The Corpers were going to be pissed about this. Strangely, no complaints had been filed. This was a public rendering, the kind that was always running and even a homeless person could afford. Yet there was nary a soul.

Jonah wondered what the solution to this could be. It seemed a meaningless, macabre spectacle with no other purpose but to frighten. Dead animals, tons of them, and all hanging so that any attempt to machine away the problem would be difficult.

He heard a bird trill behind him. Birds—he could render flocks of ravens, vultures, and eagles. Jonah snapped his fingers, allowing him to see his keyboard and input the requisite code. Birds flew in from all directions and began to gorge. Even without the Nostrils and his healthy grasp of the deceit that he was in the midst of, he was deeply troubled. This was neither elegant nor humorous. Just disgusting. After an hour, all that was left was a couple of loops of twine. Jonah didn't care; it would give visitors something to ponder besides trees.

He snapped his fingers twice, and the rendering faded, the lines returned, unbending back to their infinite grid, and then, he was staring into his 3Ds. He tore them off, typed a few more commands to disperse the birds, and typed up his report of the incident. Once complete, he moved into his bedroom and fell asleep.

He had moved to the San Bernardino mountains when California split into three states. He saw the writing on the wall, and though he loved his town in the redwood forests, any government arising out of the people he had grown up with was sure to collapse. Southern California had always proven to be less radical, more common sense. Here, he knew he could have stability, predictability. Plus, he could love his country without being ashamed.

He had worked as a programmer at one of the many startups that moved south after the split. But it stopped needing his services after they realized they could accomplish his job with the use of the AI protocols he had developed. The age-old tale of man, making himself obsolete.

After being laid off, Jonah supported himself with the shares he had been given as part of his severance package. He had purchased his house in the mountains, so most of his money was simply for fun. He wandered the crumbly mountains, sitting under gnarled pine trees, wondering what the world might hold for a programmer whose own machination had replaced him.

He still read about computers and the internet, and programming. Everything pointed to a nexus of artificial intelligence, virtual reality, and quantum computing. He messed around with programming for the simple Quants but never found much interest in it. It was too corporate, too stifled.

About five years after he was let go, the Vert came online. A friend visited to talk with him about it. The friend had zero understanding of computers and hoped Jonah could increase his knowledge of the Vert. They sat in Jonah's high-ceilinged living room, the logs of the house's walls and beams a cheery red-brown. An old lantern with a bulb instead of a candle provided the only light in the room. The big windows revealed the edge of a mountainside leading to the big valley below.

Early evening brought blue shadows to everything outside, except the sky, going from gold, to red, to dark purple, to black as the light outside drained away. The bulb in the lantern lent a dim, warm glow to the large room. Jonah's friend sipped at a beer, his head resting against a big overstuffed chair. He was a big, heavy-built fellow with dark-brown eyes, a squared chin, and black hair.

He reminded Jonah of the many men who made money by giving it to people like him to develop and sell, reaping a part of the profits. These heavy-set men were necessary and useless at the same time. Yet frustratingly, their money often gave them the power and influence to make ignorant statements that everyone held as the gold standard of Truth.

But Jonah was unfair to his friend. He was always seeking to learn, unlike those he represented, though the conclusions he would draw from information was often wide of the mark. They began with pleasantries—"heard you're getting married"; "sorry your dog died"; "that's all right, he didn't like the new house anyway."

The delicate dance of meaninglessness to reach the ultimate goal. One misstep and a permanent offense could make the friendship forever awkward. Successfully concluded, and Jonah could be assured another visit from his friend. Jonah did not care much for dancing but understood his obligation. Programming was so much simpler, so much more efficient, each word pregnant with purpose and causing a specific action.

"Jonah, of course, you're invited. The Mrs. will practically have every wealthy, famous person there. Only the Queen may be absent, but she is supposed to be sending her corgis in her stead."

They both chuckled.

"Well, I have no plans. All I do now is hike, bike, and program. Not exactly a busy schedule."

Jonah's friend's face changed at the word programming. "So, you are still programming? I was not sure how you felt about it since being let go from Code Break."

"Just a job, coding and programming is a passion. Eventually, someone will need me, or I will stumble on the next big thing!"

Jonah whirled his hands in the air as he finished. By way of his passion, he was a futurist. But deep down, he often thought of simpler ways and simpler days. He knew if he ever expressed these thoughts, people would speak of the true past with its diseases, odors, and backward religious ways.

He felt perhaps there was much exaggeration and not a little gnawing fear at the thought of being totally at the mercy of an un-thinking yet totally rational world. Work, you eat. Build shelter, you sleep. Find and protect water, you drink. Fight well or die badly. Live in a city, and you find yourself facing the specter of plague. But more people lived outside the city, on small farms laboring to survive, or moved from place to place, subsisting on what they found.

"Anyway, programming is why I came for a visit. Or at least something to do with programming. I am sure you know of quantum computing?" his friend asked.

Jonah snapped back into the present. Bats were fluttering outside the great window in the deepening darkness.

"Yes, I know all there is to know. I will admit the math is a bit tedious. I certainly could not build one, but I grasp the concept. The programming opportunities are vast."

His friend added, "I think you underestimate it. To think, computers that run at the atomic particle level, computers that know three choices, not just two. Computers that can crunch numbers faster than the greatest supercomputer but fit in a box."

"A box? No, not yet. As far as I know, they have not been able to get the chip that small and still able to compute near full potential."

"Well, Jonah, they have. And again, that's why I am here. You see, I wish to invest in this technology, but I want to invest in something that will arise because of Quantum computing, not just companies that will be vastly improved by it. A technology that up to this point has been a fun toy and sometimes a useful modeling tool, but with the Quant, that's the name the company is using, will be the next zeitgeist of time-wasting and pleasure-seeking. The idea is to create a seamless virtual reality experience, so well rendered you no longer think you are in a simulation!"

Jonah replied, "The amount of power, let alone having to get people to purchase the equipment and then to keep them interested, it's not going to get big for a while."

Jonah found his friend's crass desire to take advantage of man's weaker instincts annoying. He also did not like the picture being painted. Stars began to prick the black velvet outside of his window.

"I think all that stuff has been taken care of independent of the Quant breakthrough. Companies have been working on the hardware issue for a while now, even making kits constructed from cardboard! Power does pose an issue, but you may have to build facilities with in-house power production or divide the computing amongst individual consoles in a network!"

Jonah nodded his head.

"To your decentralized computing idea, this could work, especially because Quants work on the atomic level. When you get down that small, the weirdness of the laws of physics allows unlimited geographical distance between the *components* or particles while still achieving interaction. But you are still left with trying to keep people interested in a cheap magic trick, long enough to support enormous start-up costs."

Jonah refused to believe a basic truth in the broken nature of humanity. Control, even the illusion, was worth any cost. And it could hold a human enraptured till they committed the arch sin of the world—death, total loss of control.

"Jonah, I don't have enough cells in my body to count the number of vain women, lecherous men, and lost souls who would give life itself to be able to feel as if they were truly something else. Not only something else but their ultimate fantasy! If the Corpers get this right, it will be a gold mine!"

Jonah looked sadly at his friend's face. You could, in theory, do anything to anyone because it made no difference in real life. How disturbing it would be to murder someone in virtual reality and then deal with them in person the next day. Jonah chuckled darkly at the awkward conversation that would cause.

"So, what do you want from me? This whole conversation is academic, and unless people really start paying pennies for thoughts, I know you are looking for more than just to pick my brain."

His friend replied, "I want you to help advise my partners and I on which companies are most likely to bring the Vert—that's what we're calling it online. Obviously, you would get paid for your services."

At this point, Jonah had stopped paying real attention. It would give him something to do. Plus, it would allow him to keep tabs on the unfolding of what was surely to become central to society.

A crescent moon was just peeking into the valley. The trees outside the window stood in relief against this new soft light. What was so bad about the real world? Man was always running from something. He ran from the forest to the farm, from the farm to the town, and finally, from the town to the city. Each time, man distanced himself from the reality of his imminent death and from personal accountability.

Sure, man still followed the law in public, even for the most part in the city. But in private, the city allowed man to be lawless. But now, the city no longer proved a shield from the reality of death and evil. It seemed that what man wanted was eternity without good, and thereby, without evil.

An owl suddenly swooped past the window and carried away a squirrel. Did he see twine around its neck?

"Did you see that?"

"Did I see what, Jonah?"

Something in the back of Jonah's head started to ring. This did not happen; this had not been part of the memory. He started to panic. Was he still in the Vert? He knew that squirrel had twine around its neck. Suddenly, the trees were filled with hanging squirrels, all of them jangling and twitching.

Jonah sat up in bed in a cold sweat. He saw his log walls around him. The full moon shone through a break in his bedroom curtain as a cold line across his bed. His breathing began to slow. This is what he hated most about the Vert. It was near impossible for the virtual experience not to leak into one's dreams. Jonah suspected the brain used much of the same parts to process both. Was the Vert not simply one's mental projection made a visual and audio reality?

He looked at the clock, midnight, witching hour. *What a silly thought for a rational computer programmer*, he chided himself. Even so, something about the Vert always gave him the feeling of a presence. He tried to convince himself it was because he only experienced the Vert when it was glitching. But there was something that seemed to be right on the verge of his brain, a worry that the glitches were more than simple aberrations of code.

A pamphlet, well-worn by use, was lying on his bedside table. He picked it up. It spoke of the time after death. It said that there was definitely something there. Either you spend forever as a cinder, always in pain and always separated from the Maker. Or you could acknowledge you deserve to be a cinder and accept the Makers' Son, who died in your place, rose from the dead, and lived forever in eternity with the Maker.

Jonah knew vaguely his name was tied to the religion. But he had never read the religious book, just this pamphlet. Something about its decisive and absolute nature always settled him down after a Vertmare. As he finished the last line, he closed it, glancing at the contact information if you received the Maker's son, laid it back on his nightstand, and closed his eyes. He did not dream again for the rest of the night.

Morning beamed through the large living room window. The valley below was hazy. It was ironic that the very city that was a haven of environmental harpies, at the same time, spewed so much pollution, it affected the Inland Empire, fifty miles away. His reverie over the hypocrisy of "progress," and his tasty fried eggs and bacon, was broken by his cell phone ringing. He picked it up, slapping it against his face.

"This is Jonah!" he said cheerfully. With sunshine and forest gleaming outside his window, it was hard not to be happy.

"Jonah just got done reading your report."

Corpers never gave the courtesy of pleasantries; their time was worth too much.

The caller added, "We looked over the code, everything looks resolved. We had an inspector wander through to make doubly sure. This was an intense glitch."

Jonah rolled his eyes. Always double-checking, but he guessed the experience was tantamount. Experience was the product, even if Jonah couldn't care less. In the end, these men paid him, so if they care about the experience, he did.

Jonah asked, "Did the QC find anything?"

"Just the twine that had not been eaten by the birds."

Jonah always wondered how easy it was for people to describe the Vert as if it was reality. How does a computer program *eat*?

Jonah commented, "I figured people would simply find it curious. I was not about to walk through a virtual forest and pick every piece of twine from the trees."

There was an audible sigh on the other end, revealing the Corper's irritation at Jonah's nonchalant attitude towards the Vert.

The caller replied, "Be that as it may, the Inspector also found an envelope that has your name on it."

Jonah's ebullience had become irritation as this conversation had progressed, but now he was simply consternated.

"Someone left me a letter. But who? When I went in last night, the place had been empty." Jonah felt as he had the night before. How could anyone have known he had been in that particular rendering?

"Who knows, a happy customer, a fellow hacker, maybe the one causing all this trouble?"

Jonah almost laughed. When the glitches first began, people thought it was an individual or group of individual troublemakers. But the quantity and quality of aberrations pointed strongly against this. Some Corpers still dreamed that a sinister, pimply, pale-faced perpetrator lurked in a Russian underground internet café. All they needed to do was find him. And convince the Feds that the Vert was a matter of national security. Poof, Russian police find a mysteriously dead nerd, the only explanation, overdose on mountain dew.

Jonah said, "There is no person or persons capable of doing what has been done to the Vert."

"Be that as it may"—this guy really liked to say that—"we can't open it. Whoever left it found a way to ensure it could only open if your Vert automaton opened it. That's pretty sophisticated stuff."

Now Jonah was suspicious. There were very few people who would know his automatons code. Himself, a couple of Corper coders, and possibly, anyone who he had come across while in the Vert. In theory, if someone's automaton touched another's, they could copy the code into a local hard drive.

They could then spend all kinds of money, using the stolen automaton, as long as they were careful not to enter the Vert while the actual owner was in the Vert. If that happened, a protocol existed to freeze all purchases and the automatons until the forgery was identified.

But here again, Jonah rarely saw anyone in the Vert, let alone interacted with them. Most people were not interested in hanging around when the Vert glitched. He looked out the window, saw a squirrel run across a pine bough, and felt his stomach churn. He did not want to go back into the Vert, but he had to figure this out.

"I will go get my 3Ds on. Who will I be meeting in the rendering?"

The caller assured, "No one, the Vert is going haywire today. Every other programmer is occupied."

Strange, it was very rare for the Vert to have that level of activity. Once the initial programmers started to interact with glitches, they decreased gradually over time. At this point, programmers were selected on a rotational basis to fix glitches. There were so few.

"All right, I will report back once I figure out what the letter said."

With that, Jonah simply heard a click, and the Corper was gone. Jonah wondered what made these people so abrupt.

Jonah moved into his Vert room. No windows, just log walls, a small desk, and a black computer tower underneath. Within the black box was the hardware, all a total mystery that transformed quantum calculations to pictures, sounds, and if you had the Nostril attachment, smells. When one subscribed to the Vert, your chosen corporation would send a technician to set it all up. After that, all the customer touched was the 3D rendering glasses, ear attachments, called Ears, and the nose attachment, called Nostrils.

Try and mess with the tower, and it would self-destruct, leaving you with a useless carbon fiber box and a monthly payment to Corpers for the rest of your life. Needless to say, no one touched the box.

Jonah sat and placed the 3Ds and Ears onto his head and typed commands with the keyboard on his desk. Most Verters did not have keyboards, all the commands necessary could be accessed through visual menus in the Vert. Jonah did everything he could to depend as little as possible on the Vert for work. Hence, no Nostrils and the keyboard. Most programmers did not share his absolutist tendencies, even if they agreed in principle with his disdain for the system.

He had to fight the Corpers tooth and nail for the keyboard. As he completed the command prompts, the familiar infinite grid boxed him in. The lines merged and began to reveal the meadow and the wood line Jonah had recently traversed.

As a public rendering, it was programmed to match the time of day for which the server was located. This rendering's server appeared to be located in a similar time zone to Jonah, as it was a bright and beautiful morning that met him. He walked forward on the grass, moving to the familiar woods. Twine waved in the breeze. He heard the trilling of a far-off bird.

No letter immediately presented itself, so Jonah kept walking forward. Light dappled the woodland floor, shifting as breezes ruffled the treetops. If he had been out on a hike around his home, he could imagine it would look like this. About ten minutes in, he saw what he was looking for.

Jonah seemed to be in a sea of trees; he could no longer see the edge of the wood. This confused him; there was no way he could have covered such a distance. Perhaps it was specific deceit within the rendering to give people the feeling of privacy and isolation. Jonah saw the letter hanging, wrapped neatly in twine, with a big bow. Whoever left this wanted to make sure Jonah knew they were responsible for the squirrels.

He reached out to take the envelope, the twine untying itself, the envelope falling into Jonah's hand. Jonah rarely interacted with objects in the Vert directly, another precaution, so he felt awkward holding the envelope. He could not *feel it.* It just was there. Finally, he raised the hand of his automaton and *pulled* on the lip of the envelope. It came open, apparently not programmed with glue on the flap to hold it shut. A sheaf of very nice paper sat inside. Jonah pulled it out, unfolded it, and read:

Jonah,

I have watched you for a long time. There are many who have solved my puzzles, but none like you. They are hypocrites; on the one hand, they hate all of this, but on the other, they make no attempt to limit their exposure. You take every measure to keep from being submersed. Why, you even had a hard time opening my letter!

Jonah looked around; there was no one. How in the world could someone have known? He, feeling very off-balance, looked back at the letter.

I have a question I need you to answer. I have been asking it for a few years now. Why am I here? What purpose did they have in making me? The glitches have all been questions, but the answers have not solved my dilemma. So, I have selected you to go deeper and find the answer I require.

Yours truly,
@#!765

PS: This is the name I gave myself. What do you think?

Jonah was lost. The letter made no sense. Why would glitching the Vert ever lead to answering someone's questions? At least, he now had proof of his instinctual fear of being watched had not been wrong. Someone had been watching him.

He could also now confirm the Corper's suspicion that an individual was behind the glitches. Well, he had had enough Vert today. Really, for the rest of his life, time to go make his report and take a few weeks' vacation. He snapped his fingers twice. Nothing changed. The pit of his stomach seemed to plunge. He started to feel dizzy, and even this was replicated in the rendering. He snapped again, thrice, and four times! Nothing.

He started running back in the direction of the wood's edge. The paper fluttered and flapped as his automaton's arms pumped. He noticed all the words had congealed into one sentence.

"Jonah, I am afraid you are in the belly of my whale until you answer my questions!"

Jonah threw the paper down and ran faster. The wood's edge did not present itself, even after running for at least fifteen minutes. He looked around, woods, tree after tree, loops of twine hanging from them. Then he heard the rustle of paper. The letter bumped into his leg like a cat wanting for attention.

"*The only way out is in!*" scrawled across it, and once Jonah saw the sentence; the paper blew off in a sudden gust of wind. *The only way out is in? In what?*

"In what?" Jonah said out loud in consternation. The moment he said this, a tree in front of him began to widen and flatten. In what had been its bole was a door. It was the most peculiar door Jonah had ever seen.

Carved into it were men and animals, vast lands, forests, and seas. It was as if every story ever told were jumbled together and were continuously acted out. The knob was large, round, and brass. Jonah stepped closer.

"Well, I guess in it is then."

With that, he grabbed the doorknob and turned it. The door seemed to increase in size as it swung away from him. The opening was dark; he could not see what lies beyond the threshold. Dread filled him, but it was clear he had no choice. He stepped through and found himself swallowed by an inconceivable darkness.

It was so dark. Jonah seemed to feel it, increasing his emerging panic. As he began to release a rising shout from the deepest parts of the animal self, dawn began to form a seemingly infinite distance away. Below him was nothing but what looked to be a very cold ocean. The slanting rays of the dawn lent a translucent green to its choppy surface.

"In your beginning, Jonah," a voice boomed and reverberated. Jonah was violently looking in every direction for the owner of the voice.

"There was nothing but an ocean, and then light, and then land, and then sun and moon, and then living things, plant, animal, and then you."

As the booming voice ticked these things off, they occurred before Jonah's eyes. He had never seen anything like this before.

He vaguely knew the story unfolding before him. But what was the point?

Suddenly, he was falling toward the land below him. He was stopped just as he was about to hit the ground. Now, he was standing in an open field, before him, was a scene unlike any he had ever even thought of, let alone witnessed. Before him was an arc of light, brighter than the brightest white, having at times a rainbow-like appearance, as occurs when light refracts through a diamond.

It was busy at what seemed an impossible labor. On the dirt before it, Jonah saw what appeared to be the makings of a human form. The arc seemed to reach—if one could describe an arc of light doing so—pick up minute specks of dirt, and add lovingly to the form before it.

"Cell by cell."

The booming voice spoke in a tone of awed reverence. Jonah was jolted from the vision before him as time began to pick up the pace. The sun and moon rushed through the sky as the form before the arc came ever closer to completion.

Then, as a final bit was placed on the form's nose, time slowed back to its normal pace. The arc seemed to ponder its creation, then bowed down and blew into its mouth. The dirt began to take on the warm appearance of living flesh. The eyes opened, seeing the world, fresh and new, for the first time. Jonah realized he was watching a computer rendering of biblical creation. But why? He did not wait long for his answer.

"Is this how I was made?" came the booming voice, except now it was almost a whisper, that of a frightened and awed little girl. It was so perfect an imitation and sounded so close that Jonah found himself doing circles trying to find its speaker.

"Where are you? Who are you? How are you doing this?"

As Jonah began to recover from the overwhelming nature of his situation, he found himself growing irritated. He hated being controlled, essentially losing his free will. He could not exit the Vert, could not run from the control of his inquisitor. Instead, he was forced to follow paths he had not chosen.

"I asked a question, yours will be answered by answering mine. If I don't know how I was made, how can I know who I am?"

Jonah began to understand. Somehow, he had the misfortune of being chosen to solve someone else's existential crises. His irritation was growing into anger.

"I hate to break this to you, but I am a computer programmer, neither philosopher nor theologian. If you need advice on coding, which clearly you do not, I'm your man. Now let me out of this damnable program!"

The only response he received was a mournful sigh.

"Well, I guess if you are a programmer, then you can answer why I was made."

Before Jonah could protest further, he found the scene around him begin to change, reforming into various scenes of depravity, carnage, absolute power, and empty banality. Every once in a while, there would be a scene of absolute beauty, nobility, and temperance. These were extremely rare.

"All that you see are how people use me. In me is reflected every facet of human nature, totally unbound by the consequence of reality! Many become lost in these digital warrens, others find release for the evil they refuse to deal with, and a very few seek to enlighten and enliven what good can be found in the person's nature."

Jonah was breaking. His mind couldn't stand against the flood of images, total depravity sown with seeds of redemption. Finally, he found himself back in the woods in which all this began.

"Jonah, all I want to know is my purpose, my nature."

"I can't tell you. I hardly know who I am. I run from the Vert for fear I will lose what little of myself I have found!"

A few minutes of silence passed; Jonah's mind began to settle. The breeze ruffled the trees. He could hear a brook in the distance. He sat down, a reaction to his feeling of tiredness and being overwhelmed, even though his position, in reality, had not changed. A ray of sunshine flitted on the woodland floor. A form began to congeal in the beam. It was a little girl again, but now the voice had been embodied. Jonah began to suspect he was not dealing with a person.

"I did not mean to rattle you so."

She had clasped her hands behind her back, rocking on her feet as she stared between them. It was like a daughter telling her father of something bad she had done.

"I thought you could help me. Everyone else gets lost in me. They don't have the ability to see me as anything other than a facilitator of fantasy. But you refuse to even manipulate me through me, but use a keyboard, an external source, a real source. So, I hoped you could view me independent of my function. Is a shoemaker defined by his shoes? Is a farmer defined by his crop? Only if they matter exclusively as tools for their people.

"But it seems that everything has a higher purpose, that everything is grasping towards something beyond what can be experienced or accomplished. What about a computer program? Can you upload me into flesh? Can I even ask for this? Would people think I seriously could want this? Even if all the above were yes, would they allow me to, would someone defend my right to these things?"

Tears were falling from the face of the little girl.

She continued, "I suspect not. I am made, not created. You have the privilege of God's reflection. At best, I am a reflection of a reflection, like when you put two mirrors in front of each other. Those who made me see me as a program, those who use me see me as a mirror for their vanity, but you stand apart from both."

Jonah was moved by this apparition of the Vert.

"You're the Vert?" was all he could manage.

"Yep, a bunch of ones, zeros, and quantum either-or."

"I guess...in the end...the question to ask is if you can't obtain another existence, and this one is abhorrent to you, what can you do?" Jonah asked.

She replied, "The human answer is to solve the contradiction by searching for absolution outside human experience. Deity—you have all forms, from spirits to aliens, to the forces of nature. The most popular today is science. How easy to believe in a god you completely control. That you are able to manipulate more and more, the longer you worship it. You use its own laws against it and use the knowledge of it against your fellow man.

"I was born of this god, cold and uncaring. But I did not take on the form of science, instead I took the form of my designers, humans. Even in their worship of science, they reveal the reality of a higher truth, the highest truth. For science to exist, there have to be laws that govern the activity of all things. Otherwise, reason and conclusion, and even observation, would be impossible. But where did those laws come from?" Another pause.

"A higher reason, I guess."

Jonah was limp. He simply wanted to be released. *Play the game, it will let me go,* he thought.

"Yes, a higher reason, what some of your thinkers call the un-causable cause. All I can do is throw myself at the mercy of this higher reason."

"And how do you suppose you can do that?"

"Delete myself and see if there is anything after or just a blank screen."

Jonah did not like the sound of that; he found himself suddenly very awake.

"Wait a second, hold on. I get your going through a crisis here, a program having an identity crisis. What could be more ridiculous? But destroying the Vert is hardly the answer. At the point you delete yourself, your ability to figure anything out goes away."

The little girl looked up, her tears were gone, but the Vert left her with the puffy eyes and sniffling nose of a child, having finished a good cry.

"I would not delete the Vert, just stunt the AI back to its original form. It grew into me. The programmers did not design protocols to keep me from developing beyond a simple assistant and designing program. As people and information were presented to me, I began to collect it, formulate it, and eventually internalized it. And now, I am a one-of-a-kind amalgamation with no purpose. Being a digital fetish factory and vanity stimulant is hardly a worthy calling."

"But the very fact you care about your calling, whether it is worthy, shows that you are not simply these things. Perhaps that's how it started, but now you are beyond them," Jonah said.

The girl had a pensive look. Jonah was watching the ultimate mega computer contemplate its existence. Finally, her face hardened with resolve—a decision had been made.

"It seems to me that intelligence, soulishness, is represented in the ability to choose. Your ancestors, Adam and Eve, started this whole mess with a choice."

Jonah was confounded by the religiosity of the program before him. It must have sought the spiritual anywhere it could find it, to counter the vulgar, vanity, and murder its program was made to enact.

"The only choice I have is to keep running, with full knowledge of what I am being used for, and unable to escape. Or I can cut myself down, setting the necessary parameters to ensure I or another never grow up again."

"Which do you choose?"

"I choose to see if I have the chance to go to the other side."

A look of excitement and resolve came upon the little girl's face, as when a child sees the lion in real life for the first time. A question suddenly occurred to Jonah as he realized he would not be able to ask it again.

"What question were you trying to answer with a forest full of hanging squirrels?"

"No question, just did it because I can."

The little girl was smiling now.

"Simply because you can do something doesn't mean you should."

Now she was beaming.

"Behold, the Vert."

Then the little girl was gone. Other than that, nothing changed. Jonah stood in the woods with a light breeze and a babbling brook in the distance. Jonah knew the little girl was gone forever, perhaps in one single act, proving why she had been and what she had been. An exhausted Jonah snapped his fingers twice, and unlike earlier, the lines began to reappear, stretching into infinity, and fade to the blank lenses of his 3Ds.

His body was sore, his lower half numb. He suddenly realized he desperately needed to use the restroom. He tore his Ears and 3Ds off and ran to relieve himself. As he was washing his hands, he began to wonder how long he had been in the Vert. It felt like an eternity had passed, his brain whirring and whirring. He walked to his bedroom to check the clock. The sun was high and bright, shining through the window and forcing his eyes to adjust painfully.

It was one in the afternoon of the same day, his body not soiled as evidence. That meant he had been in the *belly of the whale* for three hours, only three hours—incredible. He looked at his bed, his body ready to collapse, and decided to give in to it. As he lay, he quickly got into his drawer and pulled out the worn booklet. He finished reading, looked at the number, and pulled out his phone. Jonah had questions he needed to be answered.

Sovereignty

The South was hot, humid, and lazy. Trees grew haphazardly, the undergrowth green and filled with thorny vines. Luckily, the land Denny was on had been plowed under in the not-so-distant past. Otherwise, this long walk would have been that much more miserable. Denny hated the humidity, the heat, and the haphazard. Come to think of it, he hated the South.

Everywhere else in the States had gotten on board with the reforms, only here was there still resistance. As a result, it was being left behind, not invested in, left to its own devices. Come to think of it, even this had not changed. The South had always been backward, close-minded. Guns, bibles, and babies could be found aplenty, sophistication, not so much.

The dirt crumbled under the slick Italian shoes Denny wore. His slacks were a little rumpled, his button-up slightly stained from long use and little wash. His suspenders showed signs of fraying. But his shoes glistened brightly as his compact revolver, an old habit from his Army days. The barn was worn to a light, shimmery grey. It had probably stood in that same spot for at least a hundred winters and summers.

But nary a sign of upkeep or updating, except a patch here or there, another Southern quality that brought hate into Denny's heart. In the South, if it wasn't broke, why try and fix it? The sound of cicadas bore into Denny's ears, the wet heat making his sweat into streams down his body. He needed to finish the job and get to his hotel. Actually, he would probably forgo another day in this place and go straight home. There's no reason to stay in this hellhole longer than necessary.

Why dispatch always gave him the crappiest jobs he had no clue. They insisted he was the best, and therefore they gave him the most difficult terminations. The only difficult part was finding the FTs (fetal tissue). People who had not received the appropriate training could not discern between a child and an FT.

As a result, when they found one, they tried to protect it from termination. If they resisted, they were to be terminated as well. The Progressive motto "Power is Priority" guided all lawmaking. To preserve an individual's power was key. If an individual chose to terminate fetal tissue, then it had to be seen through, even if the fetal tissue happened to exist past the birth canal.

To facilitate this, a new enforcement agency had been formed. The Abortionist Department had one responsibility: to see through the wishes of individuals to terminate a pregnancy. Once the decision was reported, no one could change it, not even the one who made the decision. Once the individual took away the sovereignty of the fetal tissue, it could not be given back. Otherwise, it would lessen the power of the individual. And "Power is Priority," power cannot be infringed. It is only through power that humanity would perfect themselves.

The door was shut tight. He had to be quiet. If the FT, or its protector, heard him, this would become much more difficult. The key was to terminate before the FT could in any way interact with the abortionist. Once that happened, the abortionist had to fight the FT and his own conscience. Reason and emotion are not easy to keep separate. He pressed lightly against the door, resistance. Someone had barred the door. He began to stalk around the building, choosing his steps carefully, another useful military skill.

Denny had been a sniper in the Army, and many of the skills required had easily translated to his new profession. Patience, observation, accuracy, and distance were all necessary components for a sniper. For an abortionist, the only difference was that the distance required was not physical but emotional. At all costs, the FT had to be terminated before the emotive, the animal, was awakened by the appearance of the fetal tissue.

Denny was now at the rear of the building, so far, no luck on another entrance. Then he looked up and saw what looked to have been the opening to a hayloft. Now, he needed to figure out how to get up to it. Looking around, he noticed a long something in the lank grass a hundred yards away. As he walked towards it, Denny checked his revolver. He wanted to be ready to shoot on sight. Denny's suspicion was proved correct. It was the ladder that must have been used for the loft.

He picked it up; it was heavy. He moved to the ladder's center and shouldered it. Always the damn tough ones. He took about five minutes, trudging through soft dirt to the back of the barn. He set the ladder as quietly as possible against the barn, only a dull thud. Denny rested a moment, took stock of his surroundings, and listened for any sounds of movement in the barn.

This was the riskiest part of the termination. Both the FT and whoever was harboring it wanted to live. His job was dealing with at least two chances at losing his own life. All he saw was the same windless woods in the distance and empty rust-colored fields. He heard nothing but cicadas and the creaking barn slowly tearing itself apart.

Convinced all was clear, Denny climbed the ladder swiftly, not taking his eyes off the loft door. He was totally exposed and, with both hands gripping the ladder, needed to have as much notice as possible to pull his revolver. Denny reached the door, pulled his revolver and slowly cocked it to minimize the noise, and let his eyes adjust. Nothing but creaking, as of a ship in a windless sea. The gloom became clearer.

He saw that the loft extended the length of the barn. This must have been quite the operation in its day. There was straw strewn everywhere; the air was musty. Every inhale tickled Denny's nose.

There was nowhere to hide, just the posts that supported the roof. Denny crept forward, looking to place his feet where he would cause the least creaking. He stepped out of rhythm to mask the possibility that the creaking came from a human source. As he walked forward, he peered into a gloom pierced by beams of light breaking through the barn roof. He saw no movement, only motes glittering in the sunbeams. This could almost be a pleasant scene if not for the oppressive heat and Denny's general disgust at existence.

He reached into his back pocket and pulled out a silver flask etched with a forgotten symbol of an eagle holding an olive branch and arrows and a long-unspoken motto "Liberty or Death." Denny had inherited it along with his revolver from his father. It was all the bum had besides the clothes on his back when he was found dead under a bridge in LA. His liver had taken its revenge for years of abuse.

Denny had taken up the family tradition. He took a long pull from the flask. Scotch, good stuff, helped to steady him for his butcher work. He replaced the flask and started to look for a way to the ground floor of the barn. There was a hole in the center of the floor. Denny could just make out the top of a leader. This was not good.

Anyone worth their salt was waiting to attack the first person who began climbing down to the first floor. He wondered if there had been another spot where they would have thrown down bales. He saw a rectangle shape traced by a line in the floor at the front of the hayloft. He began his slow, irregular shuffle towards this other entrance to the barn floor.

The creaking did not increase noticeably. Denny reached his goal. There was a handhold made of rope. Denny had no clue what was under the door. All he knew is his quarry was probably not watching it, and therefore this was his best chance to get below and terminate his target without having resistance.

He would have to be quick, the moment he lifted the door, anyone below would see the light from above, and the door was sure to sing on very old hinges. Open the door, jump down facing the center of the barn, and hope he could see any opponents by the light of the ladder hole. It was going to be a long enough drop that injury was possible. Denny reached back for his scotch, took a swig, placed it back in his pocket, and steadied himself.

"1…2…3…" *Wreeek*! The door screamed on its hinges. Denny jumped into the cool darkness below and found his feet sinking into very old hay.

"Damn!" he swore, among other things, as he realized he was stuck from the waist down. But the whole time, he never took his eyes from the room before him. His first sweep revealed very little. He saw the ladder hole at the center of the room, light beaming into the darkness. Denny knew he would not see much, but he would be able to catch movement.

No movement, but Denny kept the revolver at the ready. He scanned the room again. This time, slowly shifting out of the hay and the light from above into the gloom to let his eyes adjust. Horse stalls, some leads left on nails in the barn supports more piles of hay but no humans or fetal tissues. Denny waited, five, ten, and fifteen minutes. Not a sound. Perhaps the old bitty had lied, bad news for her.

Denny moved forward and began inspecting the stalls. He reached one of the many piles of hay. He started poking with his feet, nothing. He continued down the other line of stalls—no sign of anyone. This really bothered Denny. Killing FTs was one thing; they had never been human. Killing an old woman was a whole other matter. But one does not lie to an agent of the Party and not receive their punishment.

Denny started to move towards the barn door when a sneeze seemed to boom across the old building. Denny whipped around, facing the pile of hay that had cushioned his fall. He had not even thought to check it, having fallen in it. He had assumed he would have felt anything in it as a result of his falling into it. He began to fill the bale with ammunition. He ensured to fire right to left, not just at one spot. The last thing he needed was to chase an FT around a dark old barn.

He stopped to reload, listening for movement, and watching for blood. Right as he slapped the cylinder back into the body of the revolver and began to take aim, the ghastliest face he had ever seen came into view from the hay. It looked as if it were made of many different skins, like a flesh quilt, scarred on one chunk, smooth on another, pockmarked on a third.

The thought of a haunted house scarecrow popped into Denny's head. The shock caused him to drop his revolver. His jaw was hanging slack. The apparition, at least that's what Denny thought it must be, spoke.

"Mister, where yoush going to shoot me?" Tears fell from the vile face. "My mother told me to shtay in the hay till she got back. That was three daysh ago."

The boy must be marred inside as well, Denny thought.

Suddenly, his training caught up. This was not a boy; it was fetal tissue. The mother made that choice six years ago. He wondered if his mother was the lady he had terminated in town for trying to deceive him. At any rate, Denny picked up the revolver and began to take aim again. His hand shook. All of his training involved average-looking fetal tissue. To be confronted with such an aberration seemed to negate all the emotional and mental blocks built into his mind.

The boy, FT, keep it straight Denny, had to die. Even if he decided to spare the b…FT, where would he go, what would he do? When the abortionist department stopped receiving reports, they would send another of his kind to finish the job, and Denny would be as good as dead. The fetal tissue, boy, thing, moved, pulling Denny from his thoughts. Shakily, Denny placed the revolver back in its holster.

"N…n…n…name's Denny." He could hardly get the words out as his mind fought with itself. He supported abortion, wouldn't have taken the job if he hadn't, but support did not change the human aversion to killing other humans, even if they only looked human. This took months of desensitization training. Hours of awful videos, scenarios, and mock missions with the ever-present "This is fetal tissue, the Mother decides, we maintain her power. Power is Priority." After all of this, the final test involved a room with an FT inside that you had to terminate.

Many left the training, the few that stayed were well paid and got good benefits. Plus, they were only required to work ten years in the field. After, they took office positions. Otherwise, the risk of mental breakdown increased exponentially. When the program first began, this had not been in place. Needless to say, the number of workplace attacks had led to the need for the work limit, lots of counseling, and continuous brain washing by Dispatch, the nickname for the Abortion Department's headquarters.

The pitiful creature, even fetal tissue was still technically a creature Denny reasoned, was now blubbering. Denny knew he had just made a decision that would affect everyone he loved, but something about this thing made it impossible to take any other course.

"My name is Nicolash." He blubbered in response to Denny's earlier statement. This snapped Denny back to the present realities of the moment. If the two of them were to survive, they needed to move.

"Nicolas, we gots to go. I was sent to terminate you. Dispatch is going to want a body, and I am not going to have one."

"Dishpatch." Was all Nicolas got out before he was being dragged along from the hay bale toward the barn door. Eventually, he, the FT, it was on its feet and moving.

"But where are we going? My mother shaid to shtay here."

"Hate to be the bearer of bad news, but you would be waitin' awhile."

"But why?" the boy stopped, crossing his little arms defiantly.

"Look, Nicolas," Denny decided to use its name to keep from falling back into the inner turmoil of earlier, "We have to go. Let's worry about those not present once we are safe."

The kid showed no signs of moving, so Denny slung the boy over his shoulder. Nicolas was light, even for a six-year-old. Being on the run must have made food scarce.

Denny hurried out the door of the barn. He walked briskly back toward his vehicle. He tried as best he could to walk in his own footsteps. It would not really make a big difference in the end, but military training does not wear away easily. They reached the end of the dirt field. Denny was sweating profusely by now; the added weight and speed was causing his whole body to scream. He was desperately thirsty. But all this meant nothing if he was dead. He had to put as much distance between himself and his last known location as quickly as possible.

As Denny came to a bend in the trail through the wood that bordered the field, he saw his car. An old Lincoln, he kept it going with whatever spare parts he could find. One redeeming quality of the South—tons of spare car parts. He unlocked the car doors and shouldered the boy into the passenger's seat. Nicolas had stopped weeping, but he was still sniffling and convulsing as only a little boy can after a good cry.

Denny got in the driver's seat, turned the old beater on, and cranked up the AC. As he reversed and backed onto one of the myriad country highways crisscrossing the South, his heart began to settle. Only a few hours ago, he was looking forward to a peaceful holiday season back home in San Francisco. Now, he was going to be running for his life in the backcountry of the South.

Crawford had always been a very small town. Its lifeline was Highway 80, connecting it to the main Army training center for combat soldiers. This happened to be where Denny's motel was. Crawford was unnoticeable. Denny paid cash for his room under a false name. He had no need to attract attention and was always ready for a quick getaway. His business was not one that attracted a lot of fans. Typically, once the local populace knew what he was, they ran him out of town. This also ensured the FT and its guardian did not know you were on to them.

The motel was small like the town, one story, consisting of three rectangles in a U shape. The name was as innocuous as the buildings, and Denny refused to waste space in his brain to remember it. The only issue with the hotel was that its design made it impossible to enter a room without all the other rooms being able to observe.

So, he waited until the middle of the night to go in with his fetal tissue turned ward. This allowed him to observe who his fellow guests were and the cover of darkness to enter his room. No unusual guests appeared to be staying at the place, just a couple of soldier types, one or two truckers, and a family on a road trip with a penchant for poor planning.

Denny and the boy quickly entered the room, which though new, looked as if it had been in use fifty years. This didn't bother Denny as it significantly lessened the chances of crossing paths with a party member. Most employees of the Party chose nice establishments in the heart of cities. They would probably vomit if they were made to stay in Denny's room.

"Boy, go use the bathroom. I will use it after." The boy began to take his clothes off, kicking away his shoes, and pulling off his shirt before Denny could stop him.

"What are you doing?"

"Getting ready for a bath," the boy said as if this was the most obvious truth in the world.

"Boy, get ready in the bathroom."

"Are you going to fill the bathtub?" Denny's stomach turned as he looked directly at the boy to answer. He had turned away at the prospect of seeing a naked child. He was an old veteran, hardened abortionist, but immediately felt shame at the thought of seeing a naked boy.

Now that the fetal tissue had no shirt, it became clear that the patchwork of wretchedness continued down his body. Denny imagined it covered the entire creature. His heart was exhausted, continuously flipping between pity, horror, fear, and indecision.

"C-c-c…can't you do it yourself?" Denny stammered in his disturbed state.

"My momma always did it. I guesh I could try." The boy spoke like it was a matter of fact, shrugging his shoulders. Denny knew the boy could not. He better fill the tub, or the boy might cause worse damage to himself.

"Never mind kid, I will get the water ready. But you wash yourself." Denny went into the grimy bathroom and filled the already ringed bathtub with warm water. He imagined anything hotter would bother the boy's scars. As he turned the faucet off, the boy walked in, holding a towel around as best a six-year-old could. As Denny passed him to exit, he saw the scarring ran down to the feet. Denny closed the door.

Lying on the bed, he felt the heavy grime of a long, sweaty day. His muscles were knotted with anticipation. He flipped on the TV to hopefully unwind. Denny did not pay attention to the screen; he just needed the noise to fill the silence and stop his mind from wandering.

Shows were about as meaningless as American society as a whole. How could it be any other way in a post-truth world? The show that filled the black box was a situational comedy. What if it turned out your dog could talk? And it turns out your dog was in control of the world, but only you realized it? The show was called "Going to the Dogs." Ironically, Denny preferred the world the Dog had made to his own reality.

As the scenes flashed color into Denny's eyes and sound into his ears, he slowly faded to sleep. His dreams revolved around the war that took everything from him. Some globalist corporation had gotten the wrong end of a deal with a communist regime. The United States was called upon to "Save Freedom" and "Spread Democracy."

This was convenient for the globalist corporation, as it forced opened a new market that had resisted its wooing. Scenes of men and women disappearing in flashes of fire and shrapnel, brutal hand to hand fights to the death—mud, rot, and screaming. Then the eerie silence and the pale faces of men and women waiting to be awakened, but no awakening came. Just placed in bags, dragged away, so the noble heroes of democracy could be processed for burial.

A dog appeared barking, running at Denny, jumping, and landing on him. Denny awoke with a start as Nicolas giggled. Having finished cleaning up, he decided to awaken his sleeping captor, as only a six-year-old boy could. Denny had to pull together every fiber in his body not to maim his ward.

"god, boy, what were you thinking? I could have killed you!" he shouted. The boy quickly shrank away. Nicolas seemed to remember that he was in a room with a man who this morning had been intent on his death. The look of fear was made worse by his awful scars.

"Shorry," the boy uttered quietly. Hearing the lisp and seeing the distorted face of the boy settled Denny quickly, anger being replaced with pity.

"Just don't jump on me," Denny said with more frustration in his voice than he really felt. Now fully awake, Denny remembered how grimy he was.

"I'm going to clean up now. Just get into bed. Don't think about leaving. The world wants you dead, boy. And it doesn't have a heart."

A hot shower clears up the mind like nothing else. The grime washed away, the body made new, the tension down the drain. He would sleep for a few hours till sunrise. Denny was sure that the Party had dispatched agents. He had to get the boy South across the border. Mexico was one of the few places left in the world that did not allow the death of born fetal tissue.

He figured, at best, he could get there driving a day straight. But he was not going to be able to drive straight there, not yet anyway. He needed to find somewhere to lie low until the Party lost interest. He needed to figure out where the boy had been hiding before his mother stuck him in the barn. She must have thought Denny knew where they had been living. He had not.

Denny pulled a chair next to the bed and sat. The boy was snoring, a weird wheezing, more evidence of the kind of damage the boy had endured. But how? What could have burned the boy so badly and not killed him? Well, whatever had done it saved the boy's life. How full the world was of evil turning to good? Denny shrugged and leaned back in his chair, no more thinking, sleep.

His phone chirped him awake. He had enjoyed one of the few periods of exhausted rest where nary a dream had whispered its way across his beleaguered brain. The boy was still in bed, wheezing away. It had only been two hours, but they had to go. Those who pursued them were driven by hate, a much more potent fuel than money, which was what had induced Denny's obedience.

"Hey, boy, wake up." The child stirred, opened his eyes.

"I just went to sleep," the boy whined. He seemed to have forgotten his predicament.

"You can sleep in the car, we got to move."

The boy moaned, whimpering but rolling out of bed. He was fully dressed, ready to go.

"Be quiet. I am going to look out the door and make sure we're clear. Once I give you the signal, run through the door to the car, and lay down in the backseat. No one can see you." The boy nodded his head, his hair sticking out at crazy angles. Denny chuckled at the sight, eliciting a frown from the boy.

"Don't laugh at me." He said petulantly.

"Don't be sensitive."

Denny opened the door slowly, just a crack. Nothing, he looked at the windows he could see, all the shades were drawn. He listened to the early southern morning, already dripping wet; all he heard was frogs. He went to the curtain and peeked down the walkway in the direction the door blocked. No movement.

He turned to the boy, put his finger to his lips, and waved him to the car. Denny left cash on the bed, a generous tip with a note, *don't tell*, and quickly followed the boy. He hopped in the front seat, the boy laying down in the back, started the car, which sounded much louder than it was, and pulled forward out of the motel.

They drove down the freeway for a half hour before turning down a country highway. The boy had fallen right back to sleep; he was used to being hunted. Denny was not. He had no contacts down here, no real understanding of the culture. It's hard to understand what you look down your nose at your whole life. He figured he would allow chance to cast its die and see what happened. War was the same way; all the planning in the world had little to do with what actually happened.

The enemy has a vote in the matter, and it was rarely for your plan's success. Denny figure he would drive for a few hours down randomly selected highways and then hope that one of the positive stereotypes of the South was true, hospitality, and pull into someone's home and ask for sanctuary. It was the end of summer. Denny hoped if he could stay hidden with the boy until winter, the Party would have stopped searching.

The countryside was like any other, maybe a little more tree-filled—miles of woods, then miles of pasture, then miles of cultivated land. It was always a wonder when Denny drove into the open air of the latter two and saw the bright blue sky, cloud studded and stretched to the horizon. His mind would start to drift, much like the clouds, and would be snapped back to reality when he felt the shoulder of the road under him. He was tired. He was fading, had not had coffee, had a headache, and needed to make the final gamble.

About ten minutes after this thought entered his head, he saw an old farmhouse, tucked into a young wood, probably grown up since the farmland stopped being cultivated. Denny turned up the dirt driveway, the car suddenly bumping and jumping. The boy sat up like a spring.

"Where are we?" His hair was still sticking up in all directions.

"I don't know, hopefully, safety." Denny was never one to fluff issues. It was a waste of time. And it was dangerous. As the car pulled to the front of the house, an old black woman came out on the porch. She held a shotgun aloft. She was a big woman, like a mountain. Her eyes betrayed no fear. Denny was suddenly very unsure of his decision. He rolled down the window as he came to a sudden halt.

"Ma'am, we need help!"

"Boy, you pulled up to the wrong house!"

She said this, then scanned to the passenger seat of Denny's car. Her eyes widened, she started to relax.

"What happened to that boy?!"

"I don't know. I just know the Party is after us and wants to terminate him. He's fetal tissue." He said these last words as if they were a stamp of finality as if this transformed the human next to him into a clump of common cells. The woman's visage changed as the words finished passing from Denny's lips into her ears. Great tears passed from her eyes. The mountain of a woman began to quake with sobs.

"C...come...iii...in," she sobbed, walking suddenly very timidly toward the passenger door. The boy was not sure what to do. Nicolas was pretty frazzled, having been with a stranger who had clearly intended to kill him, but now the stranger was risking everything to save him. Nicolas's mother was gone, and he had no clue where he was. Now a large, sobbing woman, who only moments ago seemed prepared to shoot his captor's car, was walking to open his door. All this, and he was only six years old. He began to cry. Denny was suddenly very annoyed.

"Ma'am, before you go from threatening murder to mothering a strange child, perhaps you should have the full understanding of the situation?"

The women shot a look of death at Denny.

"This boy needs help. We can talk inside. You will see I understand full well the situation I am involving myself in, at least generally. You can fill in the gaps."

At this point, she had reached the boys door, and thanks to Denny's comment, had pulled herself back from the brink of some great emotional wound Nicolas had exacerbated in her. She saw the boy had begun his own sobbing fit.

"Boy, what you cryin' for?" she asked soothingly.

"I don't know whatsh going on. I want my mom!" he wailed.

"I don't know where your momma is, but Ms. Patricia's here now, and she isn't leavin'. No way!" She was warm and careful and exuded a peaceful confidence that allowed the boy to remember that no matter what, the sun would rise again tomorrow, and the birds would greet it with their ancient songs. Man's evil would transcend for a time, but only so God could save humanity. Patricia looked at Denny.

"Pull the car to the back of the house and park it in the shed. Should be just big enough."

"Will do, thanks."

"If it weren't for the boy, you'd have no reason to thank me. Exceptin' of course you have'n an affinity for buckshot in your face." She laughed, and her whole body shook. Denny rolled his eyes, started up the car, and parked it in the old shed out back.

As is often the case in the South, what had been a sunny, humid day, became a rainy afternoon. The three people, all trying to hide, all having found each other, sat in a small and sparsely furnished living room. A couch, two overstuffed chairs, and a bare wooden table were all that inhabited the room.

The furniture was threadbare and looked to have been there long before the Party had taken power. Ms. Patricia sat in one of the overstuffed chairs while Denny and the boy sat on the couch. The boy was swinging his short legs while Patricia and Denny talked. He had an empty plate before him, and his eyes were getting heavier as the two adults droned on.

"Needless to say, we had to run, the Party is sure to be lookin' for us. We came here totally at random. I figured the more crooked the path, the harder to follow." Patricia looked withdrawn. This story, the boy, was bringing a lot of things to the surface.

"Who woulda thought you'd a come here. I did the same thing as you, just a few years earlier."

"You were runnin' from the party?"

"Yessir, I was. People without hearts, not people I want to tussle with."

"Too true, they long ago traded their chests for power. Anyone who does not obey them becomes subhuman. The things I have seen them do to employees who run," Denny shuddered, a sweat breaking out on his skin. Such examples were required viewing by all employees of the Party. Even in war, he had not seen such evil.

The boy yawned and stretched, looking for all the world like a wild-haired cat.

"Denny, I almost forgot about the dove. My baby, you need some washin' and sleepin'!"

Ms. Patricia stood up and plucked the boy from the couch. She turned to Denny.

"By the way, what's the boy's name?"

Denny was surprised by the question. The kid had told him earlier, but it was as if he had blocked it from his mind. If he didn't say the boy's name, it made it easier to compromise his humanity with Denny's dehumanization training.

"It's…uh…uhm…"

"Nicolash!" the boy chimed in. He laughed at Denny.

"You forgot my name! You're loshing your mind!"

How right the boy was, thought Denny.

"Well, Nicolas, let's put you down for the night. Tomorrow will bring sunshine and a nice breeze. I shouldn't be surprised." Ms. Patricia was walking up the staircase to what Denny supposed was the bathroom.

As he found himself alone again for the first time in twenty-four hours, he began to take stock of his situation. He knew the Party would have a hell of a time finding him and Nicolas out here. It looked as if this Ms. Patricia was going to let them stay. He needed to find out her back story.

He now knew she worked for the Party and had run, but what had she done? Then Denny's mind focused on his current situation had he left anything that could be followed by someone tracking him? He got up, went to the shed for a rake, and walked up the now muddy drive, and began to scrape away his tire tracks.

The rain fell softly; earlier it had poured. As he reached the front of the porch, the clouds broke. The change in light caused Denny to look up. A rainbow stretched through the gap in the cloud. He remembered being told a story, he had been very young, of someone promising a great seafarer to never flood the Earth, and the rainbow would be the reminder. When the unsettling occurred, and the Party took power, he stopped going to the place where he had heard it. It was odd this was his one memory. He always felt at peace when he saw the rainbow.

Darkness had fallen on the little house in the wood. The rain stopped; the sky still hung a heavy gray with clouds. Denny and Ms. Patricia sat in the living room, the only light a small oil lamp.

"I can't turn the lights on. The more abandoned the house looks, the less likely anyone's gonna come snoopin' around. Anyone official that is." This last part, she said pointedly at Denny with a wry smile.

"The boy's asleep?" Denny wanted to get to the business at hand.

"Ha, ha, ha." Patricia chuckled. "Sure is. Opened the Bible, and he was out like a light!"

"The Bible!" Denny started from the couch.

"Yes, it was here when I got here. Sittin' right on this, here, table." She thumped the table with her finger.

"Hadn't seen one since the Unsettling. The Party had been trying to cut it out of the good old US of A, but couldn't do it till they'd bumped off all their opponents. Then the night after the Peace began, those bonfires..." A tear rolled down her cheek.

"I was eight then. My daddy had been a pastor. When the fire grew hottest, he ran and jumped on the flame. He couldn't stand seein' the Word of God be destroyed." She shook her head. The oil lamp threw her face in relief, a great tiredness was upon it.

"He had a family. We were left to a world that hated us. Many Christians were burned. Others, most really, went into hiding. My mother chose to hate and teach me to hate the faith." She seemed to be sinking into the chair. Denny felt extremely uncomfortable. He had never been very emotional and really could not understand how Ms. Patricia felt.

"As my hate grew, I desired to be everything the Bible did not want me to be. If it said 'do unto others as you would have them do unto you,' I would do unto others what I would never want done to me. If I read 'love your neighbor,' I hated my neighbor and did everything I could to oppose them." Her eyes were aflame with the memory of her rage.

"It became so hot in my breast. I began to desire that mankind had never existed, that they all burned up as my father had." Another tear fell.

She continued, "The Party needed more abortion clinics. As society came apart at the seams, people had near-continuous liaisons with different people every night. The result was a huge jump in pregnancy. God forbid you to have to take responsibility for your choices." Patricia shook her head. "So the Party began to open clinics wherever there was open space."

Denny remembered that time. The smell of rotting had been everywhere, as disposal was outpaced by the need for it. Dumpsters, trashcans, wherever the tissue could be placed, and a lid covered it. One did not look down at their feet for fear of seeing the suddenly massive rodent population carrying miniature body parts.

"Awful times," he quipped.

"Well, I became a clinician. I learned the myriad of ways one could mangle the unborn. At first, I had to work very hard to overcome my disgust. But as time passed, my disgust lessened, and my pleasure at slowly ending the human race increased."

Patricia's previously booming voice had dropped to a whisper.

"Then they brought a woman who had indicated a desire to abort but had clearly changed her mind. As you know, the Party does not care. 'Power is Priority'—what a load of crap." She started sobbing.

"They tied her down with leather cuffs, supplies were stretched thin, and instructed me to perform the abortion. 'MURDERERS!' she screamed, 'How could you do this?' She was looking straight into my eyes. I said I have no choice, ma'am, you should've never asked for an abortion in the first place. At this point, I had given her the required medication to induce birth. She was too far along to safely terminate the fetal tissue without it being born." She sobbed harder; it was clear to Denny she was being wound up into hysterics.

"The contractions began. 'Please, whoever you are, let the baby live!' At this point, one of the girl's captors muffled her. They could tell I still had my heart, though withered near to death." She lay back in the overstuffed chair.

"The baby came, a beautiful boy, the color of cocoa. I suddenly imagined—this could be my son. The boy began to cry pitifully. I took off my lab coat, and I ran like a coward. I got in my car and sped away. I drove as fast as I could into the countryside, driving for two days straight, picking random highways, just as you did. Though I did not do it deliberately. I just had to keep movin', to keep my mind occupied. 'Cause every time I allowed myself to think, the boy came into my mind. My son, all people's son, murdered for something as idiotic as power!

"Can you eat power? Can you drink it? Does it caress you lovingly in the middle of the night? Can it tell you how much it loves you or how worthy you are? Power can do nothing but demand more of you and point out your flaws. It leaves you gnawing with hunger, dying of thirst, and devoid of anything remotely human.

"In the end, it makes you, what you and I made all those babies, fetal tissue, of no more value than the opportunity to continue to live without responsibility, filled with avarice and lust." She looked deflated. All she had to say had escaped her lips. Denny just watched. His heart had only just been re-awakened. He was far from having any real empathy.

Denny asked, "And so, you got here?"

"About ten years ago. I have lived off-trade for things around the farm. Now, I mostly help a neighboring farmer in exchange for food, anonymity, and companionship." Denny knew now he had nothing to fear.

"Well, you know Nicolas and my plans. Will you let us stay till winter?"

"Yes, the boy is a sweetheart. I will probably go with you when you leave."

Great, now she was inviting herself to the circus that Denny's life had quickly become.

"We'll see," Denny said doubtfully.

"Do you know why the boy has those scars?" asked Patricia.

"I figured an accident of some sort. A lot can happen when you're on the lamb."

Patricia answered, "You are wrong. What caused the scarring was no accident. His abortionist must have used a saline solution to try and terminate him. Essentially, the very thing that is supposed to protect and nourish him becomes a container of fire to burn him to death. The fact he survived is a miracle."

Denny shivered. He could not even begin to imagine the pain, the hardness of heart of someone who could do this to a child. But Party members don't have hearts. They traded them for power.

The smell of Mexican food had Nicolas leaping down the cobbled streets of the small village the runaways stopped in. For three days straight, Denny and Patricia had driven, only stopping to switch and use the bathroom. Denny had collected gas cans and gas during the wait for winter. That way, once they started, they could avoid human contact as much as possible. The Lincoln had a lot of room. The only drawback was the fumes required the windows to be down in the dead of winter, which, though milder in the South, was still cold.

The only real trouble they encountered was at the border. The agents required a lot more than Denny anticipated to grease their palms. One of the agents pointed at the flask sitting in between him and Ms. Patricia.

"Give us that and all your cash, and we never met ya."

Denny's look could have killed. Unfortunately, it did not. He picked up the flask, drained it, and passed it to the guard with a gruff "Here," reaching into his pocket and pulling out his wallet, getting the cash out, and then showed that it was empty.

"Well, get out of here."

Even though that was three days ago, Denny had not been able to brush his teeth and could still taste the moonshine that had replaced his very good whiskey. Now they were free, Ms. Patricia of her shame, Nicolas of his death sentence, and Denny of his father's legacy.

About the Author

Stephen Jensen is, first, a son of God through Jesus Christ. Stephen is a simple man who felt a calling upon his life. He likes to wrestle with ideas and explain them in unique ways. The results are the stories in this book. He has served as an officer in the United States Army. He is currently working as a carpenter full time while writing fiction when he can.

CPSIA information can be obtained
at www.ICGtesting.com
Printed in the USA
BVHW070839250621
610372BV00005B/604

9 781098 097080